STONE THE MONSTERS, OR DANCE

SPECULATIVE POETRY
WITH AMBITIONS OF MENACE

KEN POYNER

Print ISBN: 9780578948089

Front cover photo by Sean Thomas

Rear cover photo by Simone Fischer

Author photo by Karen Poyner

Barking Moose Press

www.barkingmoosepress.com

Credit is due to the magazines below which originally published many of the pieces contained within this volume, occasionally in slightly altered format.

Alaska Quarterly Review

Attention Please

Black Fly Review

Blue Unicorn

Calliope

Cincinnati Poetry Review

Colorado-North Review

Contact II

Croton Review

G.W. Review

Goblets

Greensboro Review

Hiram Poetry Review

Iowa Review

Jam To-Day

Laurel Review

Nebo

New Mexico Humanities Review

Newsletter Inago

Ohio Journal

Old Hickory Review

Old Red Kimono

Panhandler

Poet and Critic

Poet Lore

Poetry Now

Proof Rock

River City Review

Sequoia

STONE THE MONSTERS, OR DANCE

Prey

ABSOLUTION

The flowers are beginning to look like you.
Each day you have run your fingers through their roots
And now one sticks your tongue out at you.
Another bats your eyes. A third
Leans back and strokes your double chin.
You stare horrified as another pulls your hair
Down about your forehead. Furious,
You try to pry your fingers out of the soil.
Contentless pain shoots into your arms and the fingers stay.
Flowers lace the shoes on your feet,
Others sprout your Sunday gloves. Your toes
Have crawled clandestinely into dirt. Flowers
Lovingly snap your knees, bend your neck.
The garden smirks at you and produces
At each appropriate place the lines of your skin.
By noon, your back has begun to twist after the sun.
In the front yard, a string of petals
Is raking leaves, is eyeing your wife
Through the geraniums placed at the kitchen window.

NOAH (i)

All afternoon you've been testing the boards,
Looking for leaks, stamping the flooring in place.
You've scared a quarter of the animals to riot,
Knocked a deer, cross-mated when we weren't
Keeping good enough watch, into early birth
And the mess is mine to clean when, time short,
There are other duties. You've shaken the railings
I think of every stall. I tell you,
Yes, the waters seem to be going down,
If it will save you from another fit
Of convincing me, of listing your proofs. How many
Birds you've sent off in just the last two weeks
The world will never know: your madness
I hope in a better time you and I
Will hold to ourselves; I hope
That your sons have not seen. Somewhere
In the very bottom, underneath the stores,
There is a seepage and the must-smell
Is terrifying the deeper you go,
And we can't get to it. You try
All the hinges on the doors,
Swing open to ocean, waves higher than sight.
Yes, it's been long enough. Dry land is the desire
A man might have that his neighbor's grandsons
Have fertile wives. A few more days
And we'll be slaughtering the lesser beasts;
Neither I nor your children will forgive you
The times you chase after their wives.

I talk often of letting the lions loose
In the underdeck, of doing anything
That would quicken us, and it's not an idle thought.
Close the portal and come to bed.
You'll babble half the night of the physics
That will leave us stranded on rock,
Yet believing is adequate for me: I'd like
To get to sleep. You check one more deck,
Drive a new nail. All night I feel us lowering
The waters breaking on shores, this terrible arid
Smell, the desert everywhere, the bastard species dying of thirst.

THE BELIEF IN PROGRESS

There could be greatness coming.

A great people. A race that somehow

Fits more likely. A few anatomical differences,

A few behavioral changes beyond today's model.

Close enough to us that one can feel

Empathy, that - could the thought be

Not quite vulgar to them - one of theirs

And one of ours might mate. A race

Of slow movements. Tall, with huge

Deep-set eyes. An ability to feel the wind

On a face and suspect that it is wind.

Little hurry to get out of a thunderstorm

Unless there is some practical reason for not getting wet.

An order of mind that knows that mutually

Antagonistic and necessary propositions are generally

The normal course of events. Gracile fingers.

An utter lack of anger. An appreciation of line

That carries to even the most mundane, the ugliest,

That makes senseless beauty. A full two feet of greater

Stride than we, master of their own numbers.

Prayers that could be public documents.

Think of them restoring the earth, resurrecting.

Think of them looking back on us with a reasonable

Accounting for our limitations, granting us quaintness.

The power to create food out of air, to make

Even the crows peaceable. The poise

To flatten the waters, to bring speech out of trees.

Browless, but not unkind. Think of them

As free of the machine as the article once manufactured.

Think of them passing across a table the salt.

REPORT AND SUMMARY ON THE CAUSE AND RESULT OF THE FIRST USE OF TACTICAL NUKES

We worry the trees at hillside
May be a problem. Oak, poplar, birch,
Each stake proving a nemesis to machinery,
Each a cover. Many will not get
To the top. The leaves are damp,
The footing will be poor. Perhaps
The ground is mined, a battery
Overlooks from the opposite slope. It is
Not that I am afraid. There must be
Some better way of putting the place
On our side of the map. The wind
Tears through gray branches. More leaves
Fall and I think even the Druids
Have given up the land. Small feet
Race ungainly on narrow paths.
Dark is coming and our small party
Is the bravest of a nation of bests.
No life is too proud to find death mechanical:
Balloons on the board at the carnival dart throw.
A star stumbles to the top of the hill;
The evening will be clear; the moon
Should not be far behind.

We have killed a great number of squirrels.
Splinters were more a problem than
To a man anyone expected.
The land is our land.
Go around.

THE 1938 HURRICANE

I am a mark of east and west.
From the leaning posts of my iron gate
Directions are known.
Otherwise, there are thin huts,
Shacks, houses –
All weather beaten, animal scented.
From them to get to anyplace
You must be an outsider – so they
As well as the water and trees
Seem unbearably strange.
My points are exact,
My erosion slow
And as descript as hail storms.

Who could know
Bitten by sea surge, rained out,
Coffins would float?

MAKING LOVE ON VACATION IN HAWAII

Snow impacts on a land already subdued.
The eaves are preparing for collapse.
At the edge of the forest dark shadows
Contend for terror with the cold, the quiet.
Groaning windows pull you to exhaustion about the house.
The back door open, wind plays
With ice crystals in your hair. South, warm against animal flesh,
There are rabbits, a fox curled in the hollow of a log.
Why are you masking pride in your predatory traits?
Crouch. Gray teeth ready themselves at the door frame.
Your damp muzzle folds in mastery beneath your arm.
Wake up. Wake up.

OZ

Beyond some physical point the road
Is no longer the path of Dorothy and Toto,
But familiar dirt road. At home, the gate
Is open and through to the back door
You bound over loose foot stones.
From the window three farmhands
Leer at you, idle males, your small anatomy
Hardly more than a mouthful. There is
So much to be done. No one complains
Of the dog, its vicious nature, its desire
Of the cat. You twist your arms this way
And that, try to sway your hips:
The tinman, the scarecrow, the lion save you
From the pigpen so as not to see so much
Potential go to waste. Like to like opposed
You are the object the lady next door
Worries of. In your room, the shade
Up, the light behind you,
You undress slowly, inspect the straw
About your skin, the tin of your veins
The soft down of fur along your spine.
The farmhands take you in like a manatee,
Watching a thing cellulose, predictable,
Each of them struggling at the back row for plot.
Your body is the wizard's gas, the fire,
The organ voice. Inside, you seek to work
The right levers, to keep your power intact,
To not let even the dog know that behind
Some curtains there is nothing at all.

THE ATLANTEAN CATASTROPHE

They thought it could not happen. They hung out clothes,
Bought the newspaper for the grocery store ads.
They worried that the girl next door
Liked to sunbathe far out in the yard,
Already filled a bathing suit moderately well,
Could, in a few years, have all the wrong boys
Driving through the neighborhood, have the husbands
Washing windows. They thought
Hem lines were going up again. They thought
They were paying too much, that those
Who didn't produce were receiving too great.
They thought that getting old was basically
A sexual problem. They thought that clothes
Were made too cheaply, that five washings
Would do in a new shirt, three a good dress.
They thought that eating was a social affair.
They tried to make it through intersections
Just before the opposing traffic had its turn.
They watched parks disappear. They moved
Up in their jobs, but not as fast
As people with an 'in'. They complained
Of doing all the work, and getting no credit.
They thought the local council could solve
The problems of national defense, and that
The national assembly could quicken trash pick-up.
They thought that getting married and getting pregnant
Was the natural order, but had it happen
So often in reverse that no one found such

Entirely unnatural. There were grumblings
About the thickness of shopping bags,
The impudence of workmen, the morality
Of neighbors, the tight fit of shoes,
The few things that could be done with one's hair.
They voted like leaves and stems in the fields
Demanding sun. When the water rose
Two hundred feet at coastline those
Who had bought the wildly advertised oceanfront homes
Thought damn the little savings I made
Not taking out storm insurance. A woman
Miles inland, at the foot of the water's breaking
Turning from hanging out her fresh clothes, thought
All her clothes, all the clothes. I'll have to wash
Them all again, and not enough detergent in the house.

THE FOX

She turns her head one way and then the other and
You are driving the carriage. She speaks softly,
Sounds like a woman in a well, is all lips,
Tongue, the hint of teeth. A bit of hair
Has come across her forehead, advances
On the eyebrows. She doesn't wear
Too much makeup. She looks forward
From the back of her skull. There is
A blue point angling slightly away
From each eye. Not blue eyed. Brown.
Dark hair, not blonde. Her legs, firm,
Aware beneath the lap blanket, hardly move.
You pull back on the horse's reins,
Tap the side of the floorboard with your whip,
Hold onto your cap with one hand for the wind.
She wears black gloves, long, above
The elbow. Her shoulders barely tilt with breath.
You scrape thick workman's boots against the base of the seat.
A half-hour and she is home, a speck of light
On the second floor. Transformed, you turn around a birch,
The fowl still clamped in your jaws,
Still struggling, the memory of the cook's
Cold broom coming by, barely missing, hard
In your skepticism like wicker, chasing you.
You pass in and out of strange smells,
Bristle at half-heard sound, consider
Letting the done-in bird go, leap a patch of leaves,
Even with the predator's teeth in your spine

Thinking this is better. She puts out the light,
Liquifies in bed and the man knocks at the door.
She has not put up her hair in hope.

UNDERSTANDING

At first I could not turn off
The kitchen light. Flick the switch
And nothing happened. Sixty watts,
It hung by the ceiling, spreading itself
Thin as sheet ice, taking in the whole
Of the room, giving the gift of shadows.
A moment later it was the bathroom.
Standing on the sink I unscrewed the bulb
And it was worse: no heat, but the bulb
Live in my hand spoke of light. The wife
Could not keep from letting on
The lamp by the bedstand and though
The cord is in my hand it still gleams.
Watching, by the last crack of openness,
I could see as the door fell almost shut
That in the refrigerator the light pounds
Always and I worry the health
Of our food. In the garage the light
Came on all by itself and in desperation
I broke the bulb with a marble: the illumination,
A cluster the size of a fist, rolled
Idle about the concrete floor and to be
Out of its way I went back
Into the house. The place is
Nothing but light, and cutting the breaker
Has done no good. Under blankets,
Cluttered in darkness, the wife, children
And I wait for what must come next,

For the ordination. Out from the edge
Already the youngest daughter is inching,
Letting the brightness brush against her arm –
Too soon she will be up and dancing
Naked in brilliance, casting shadow
Of pure, white ash. I need rather
Take the gun to her first.

THE PARAPLEGIC

He sleeps against his dream,
Coughing dust. Two arms
Spin into his vision, beating
To tortured flight.
He hangs between them
Singing in a bird's passive coo.
Hawks rise above him,
Screaming away into cloud banks.
Starlings below shudder,
Diving from his horror into the brush.
He spins lower, hoping to land.
On a winter-stiff beach
Girls in immaculate white gowns gaze up,
Hearing the rustle of his fingers.
One steps away, and another,
And they run – a great herd of white gowns,
Rattling like chain-mail, inland.
Except one. She stands
With her face turned into his pounding chest,
Her mouth sprung hideously open, her throat
The black of dreamlessness.

Sand rushes closer.
He arches his toes, bends his knees
To land, watching
The girl grow larger, whiter.
In bird whispers he speaks.
The arms

Twist and stutter, jerking.
The boy between them scrapes the ground
And rises, lifts over the girl's blonde head,
Her wide, black throat,
Empty air
Rushing through his fingers like chatter.

The arms rage, pulling him higher.
Only the boy knows how soon
He will learn to work the knife in his toes.

THE ORIGIN OF SPECIES

An hour before supper, and an hour
After – and I think you merely
Are working a way out of peeling potatoes,
Drying glasses, clearing away. Last night
It was the hawk; this evening birds
From the flimsiest material. It won't hold,
And I catch you looking over your shoulder –
Fixing me as I work in the kitchen,
My frame in the window as I lean over the sink.
Steam off the stove, and you're in to wash up.
I place the dishes in the pan and you're out again,
Fashioning claws and bare abdomens, the sense
Of smell and quartz eyes. I lay utensils
In unlined drawers, dress glasses against open wood
And there's a houseful of chores you could do.
All night your creations are howling, scratching
The shingles, testing everything I've put in the garden.
Whenever I open the door they try to get into the house,
Have the cunning to wait under the steps,
Race for the small crack of air. I could want
A mate whose hands were put to stable use.
Today is no different. Before dinner
You get to an edge of the yard, squat down
To make the wolf; leaving the table
A mess of overturned stock and every sort
Of household item, you go out
And put together the rabbit. My chores done,
Having set most the night against

Washing, drying, putting away, I make an excuse,
Slip out the pantry door, listening for new,
Directionless fear. Hands still red from dishwater
I give the rabbit speed.

ABSOLUTE MORALITY

You do not have to kill in order to collect the bounty.
Very quickly, in the dark, on your stomach,
Licking the air for scent, you can move
Like dew shadow to the side of a man's bed –
At the outskirts of a camp, or even in center
Providing the proper escape route, your knife
Faster than sound cleanly brushing the side of the neck.
A minimal loss of blood, a sackful of ears.

GEOMETRIC DESIGN

Luckily there have always been adequate children.
One comes to understand that those who don't comprehend
The needs or methods of population control
Breed more than those who do, produce
Children who breed quite naturally,
Without thought, character, or preplanning.
There are always enough children.

When it was that Luther first got the idea I can't say.

He was out one morning adding to his barn
A third story, a shed almost, with a platform.
Three days he spent, and the fourth
He took up the first child – a boy
Six or seven, fair-headed – held him
One hand just under each arm, picked him up
Chest high and like tossing a shot-put
Put him out into air, an arc that
Quickly came to ground: the boy
On the pack-earth in front of Luther's barn
As dead as stone. Not many of us were around,
Only the immediate neighbors; but in the morning
The crowd had doubled and Luther took three children,
Girls all, and put them through the arc, one
Having to take the flight twice,
Closed up his barn till evening. After supper

We gathered and there were dozens, couples
For miles around bringing their children,

21

With community-property children wandering about
Waiting their turn – childless families
Standing at the front of the mass, gazing up.
He launched nine, few having to take the trip
More than once. The crowd was well after midnight
Dispersing. All week the numbers grew,
Children ran about like ants,
Wanting to climb up and try
And Luther sent hundreds of them out,
Let them buckle in the early summer air.

Then one caught. A girl, five or so,
Spread her arms, sucked in atmosphere,
Drifted once above the crowd and landed
Fifty yards away. The next Luther threw down –
But that one caught, a boy, soared
In a loop, lighted atop Luther's shed.
That was the last for the evening – yet
Next morning it was the same. Three
He sent out, and they flew as though
They knew nothing else: gliding even farther,
Adding positive locomotion, circling
As in a shaft of rising air. The man
Locked the place up, went to his house,
And though we gathered in the evening –
As vast a body as usual – he would not come out.

We beat the door, looking in all the windows,
Caught sight of his wife doing dishes
And rattled that pane. There were still
Thousands of children left. The barn was padlocked

And we sent for a maul. We don't know
Whether to burn him out and force him
Up to the shed, or to let one of our number
Break into the outbuilding, climb to the perch.
Children are scaling the man's roof,
Clinging to the gutters, jumping off
And landing a tangle of limbs in the shrubs.
A child falls at my feet like window putty and I can hear
I think from the caged dark inside his house Luther,
His masochistic breath as he pushes furniture to brace the door.

KANSAS

The cats are whispering in the garden.
Their long, thin voices drift in our bedroom window
Like dust. The geraniums have placed themselves
On the kitchen sill, demanding full sun.
It is not like them.
Last week, at their tea break,
The horses demanded a spot of brandy to go in.

I gave it to them.

The wheat in the North field
Has grown under the fence and is heading
For the highway. Harvest must be a slaughter.
This morning two of the dogs stole
One of your boots, dragging it west,
To the neighbor's. I found
One of McClellan's socks in the kennel.
I cannot get the cows
To lock up at night. Husband,
It is getting out of hand.
The corn has taken the hoe and hidden it.

We are up to no good.

SACRIFICING THE VIRGIN

She struggles against the rope
Piercing her ankles. The stone
Altar against her back
Burns. She is its moss.
Moisture runs across her stomach.
She is naked immodestly.
She has kept herself clean,
Guarded herself Godly,
Protected the rights of one, specific man
To make men in her.
The rounds of her womb
Have waited almost as long
As the proximal gate.

Unsure of God's need
For the soot of virgins, she twists
Against the wrist bindings, arches
Her back and
Howls. The knife
Dives deep in her chest,
Cuts through the breast
And runs round and round
The heart. Celibate
By God's command, the priest
Carves the thick mammalia, pulling the heart
Like a string until it hums
And slips from his hand.

She waits in a long gold hall naked,

Sweating along the inside of her thighs
Unaware her heart lies on the ground,
Her womb is burning, the priest
Chants. The Kingdom of God
Unfolds on all sides. One door
Along the hall is half open.
On the frame by two red ribbons
Hangs the first night's black satin gown.

SALVAGING THE ARTS IN A MEDIUM-SIZED COMMUNITY

The audience in evening gowns and tuxedoes
Waits at the edges of their seats as the orchestra,
Bowties and tails, completes the overture.
Red velvet curtains, light reduced to minimum,
The stage holds itself firm and unalterable and the villagers
Dance on their way to the vineyard.
Hilarion storms leaden in depression.
The house settles against velour cushions
And has patience the piece will end. Giselle,
Albrecht, Myrtha leap and twine and pull
Themselves through number after number – better talent
Than average, though not superior.
The Wilis fling themselves like volatile vapor,
More than mere exuberance, art in suspension,
And the prized finale is coming. Men and women
From their places slide forward. Thousands
Of dollars-worth of lights and props
Stand spurious about the hall. Giselle, exhausted,
Stumbles back along the floor, working
At the buttons of her costume,
Pulling methodically the gown's bodice: mechanism.
Men and women bring damp hands together,
Boundless applause. Across the stage naked dancers careen,
Slowing at spotlights. The audience
Stands – pointing, smiling, commenting on the best.
Barely off the stage the ballet's artistic director sits.
It is the largest house he has ever seen.
He was certain: anyone can fling nudity at a crowd, but this –
This is the humility the most dependable patrons crave.

IN THE LAND OF THE GIANTS

You saw them coming but would not
Fall back into the house. At such distance
They were but dots on the land:
Small and specific. It does not take long
For them to grow to something unmanageable.
You stood on the porch
And saw the stamping over the hills,
Biologic motion beyond the best in us.
Their huge shoes left our countryside
Torn and flattened, cultivation nothing
But mash, the work of lifetimes
Mere gravel. By the time they had drawn
Even to our house you were no longer my man.
Open to sight, your body but another part
Of the land underfoot – hands right
Angles, legs complimentary – you waited
For the matter to descend
And make a bubbling of meat and bone.
Now that they've passed by
I can hear your obscene screams
Racing after their huge and apathetic backs.
Son-of-a-bitch: I wish for sin
You would merely turn salt. Husband,
Come down from the roof!

GARANU

This land is a grandson's forest,
Grown full with toothless tigers,
Mad hatters still at factory work.
Trees enclose the day's size,
Restrict it to a compromisable deity.
Fairies and elves lounge on rocks
As a young man still seeks Alice,
Counseling with the grin of the Cheshire cat.
The boy moves heavy with grace,
Alive with the utensils of his search.
His hands more tactile
Than a grandson could grow
Mimic leaves, turn to speech.
His chance to outgrow a house
Gleams back at the smile of the cat,
The dust of Alice's dress
Catching time in a useless position.
Openings in the trees break the day's fast –
Flood the invisible with light,
Turn dull half-believed things into nothingness.
(My dreams get the best of me.
It is they who wake,
The pattern of me dissolving,
Turning a cloak of memory
Pulled about the face of a vibrant continuum
More powerful and carnal than any scrap I am.)
The boy holds out his hand,
Would rather rain settle the dust
Than sun highlight it.

CATS AND SIX LANES

There is a smell to the other side.
Something there is desirable.
Something there is desirable
Or this barrier would not have been built.
The blurs come and go:
Mechanics almost unseen, wanting only
To cause me to hold my pride
Like an empty belly and turn back.
The arch of my spine will not have it.
Gray light falls out of the darkness
And the air roars past.
Beneath me grass gives way to gravel,
The sandy feel of masters.
I am so close I am static
With the passing of each object –
The violence of light and sound,
The jet of gas. Stoic, the edge
Is solid, smooth: a thing
Not to be run upon – but I race,
Crouched in my best crouch,
Feet padding the flatness beyond grace,
Eyes a tight beam of amber.
I am a line between two points.
I am a flying thing.
I am the hunter
So close to his prey
The prey is frozen.
I am the movement

Of a thing so quick
It leaves only sight of itself.
I am the speed of death.
I am the dark beast
Seen only as the blur that brings an end.
I am.

THE HORRIBLE PRAISE

The dragonfly is as big as a small plane.
You push aside a blade of grass with both hands
And the ants are so large you could saddle them,
Replace the horse. This morning everything
In your house seemed usual, in place.
Opening the drapes, the trees were as broad
As factories, the flowers larger than clouds.
You put on your jeans and flannel shirt, expecting
Work ahead. Your door steps were normal height,
But the gravel walk had bloated,
The stones were three times the size of a man,
A path through them taking half a day.
A small stream has become insurmountable obstacle;
Street curbs are new consternation; and
The shadows of birds overhead hold unknown chill.
Slowly, out of the houses sunk in the grass,
Others are climbing, in groups of twos
And threes moving through gardens as though
Through forests, skirting rain puddles as though
They might be lakes. Six stories tall
A housecat runs past and you hide
Under the edge of a maple leaf. In the road,
Against a curb, property owners seem to gather
And you are making your way there, the question
That will decide how you handle this miraculous change
Forming itself on your miniscule lips: whether
There has been a shrinkage or an enlargement.
You'd feel yourself capable of anything

If you had had to climb out of bed using rips of huge sheets,
Had fallen mite out of your nightclothes,
Had had to slide belly first under your home's massive front door.
You rattle the change in your pocket,
Still can hold in your palm three quarters,
A dime and a penny. Your clothes still fit
And as long as they do there are a lot of things
For which you are going to be easy prey.

THE CREATION OF EVE

A new spectacle I do not need.
Putting limits on all the others
Has pulled me beyond what You might have intended.
The place is filled with howls and shrieks:
Its presence is best when seen from above.
I can hardly keep myself clean for the filth,
Clear a small space to occasionally lie in.
To be forced to share with an addition
What order I can make of this
Is horror enough; there will be extra wants
And with claws so poor and legs
Not crafted to power, I will fail,
The contract for the three of us will be soap
At Your hands. The beasts beneath me are an equal;
One more task will break a man.
But if I must accept this animal,
Draw in the oddity and give it coeval volume –
Let me have one edge, one point
To drive the tenant with,
To hold supreme like lease and lading.
Give to me, on occasion, of my schedule
And choosing, out of her time
Nine months of the year.

THE INTERSTELLAR ASTRONAUT RADIOS A DEAD EARTH

Home becomes ever larger.
What was perhaps the thought
Of a room, with certain individuals gathered,
Becomes easily the house, and then the street
Where the house lives, a subdivision, and a city.
Then state and nation, a world. Difference
Measured against the occurrence of meteors
In open space is nothing. Not even
Speaking a common language, any man comes from home.
Slowly, my bones deteriorate.
I take my exercise, eat what is best for me.
My loneliness is the desire
Of water for the sea bed. I have read
Everything I was allowed to bring with me.
I have seen every star there is. I watched
One small world and its spinning mate
Until I could watch only the distance
Down which it waits. I walk the length of this craft
And think of the hands that have touched its metal –
Men and women in white jackets,
A full five fingers, two arms, the vortices of mouths.
Home will be the length our kind can reach,
The air it is willing to breathe.
I reach too far. How honored I am,
How much the Chosen – against colliding galaxies,
And novae, and the failed plots of hydrogen fires –
Strikes me like the flat of a carpenter's best hammer.

I spend a great deal of time
Counting my appendages, noticing how on the body
Down blooms, the follicles and sweat glands,
How the tongue feels when it expects no business.
I am a reflection of the soil, moon seasons,
An evolution even of stone, and salt water.
I come out of the sun, and my one wish
Is to return. Do not worry about me.
Take care of yourselves.

THE MAN WHO LOVED TO MURDER SMALL DOGS

Do not misjudge it:
Power is not the pleasure.
Dominion is an easy task,
Accomplished almost by mere legerdemain.
With such great advantage
I cannot but be the master
Of a multiple of things. I am
That which achieves – my arms
Spread over the earth and the earth
Is mine. My purpose and demand
Is much more: my blade
Over the heart, diving through flesh –
The face of the beast, the failure
Of struggle, the simplicity of the body.
It is all there is. I go on:
The blood worries, the kidneys
Accept, the penis flies erect, the muscles
Contract and relax, the stomach gathers
To its purpose oblivious. The thing
That was with the body before me
Is no longer amongst us.
I am the marvelous machine.
I am not dead yet.

THE PATRIOT

The family next door has been again to the movies.
I think this month they were watching
One night a week the same picture –
But I could be wrong. I'm sitting on the porch,
A beer and not a light on, when they make the driveway –
All the noise of a circus, their chests thrown out
And a certainness of step real people don't have.
I'm afraid it was the war movie again.
Tomorrow the father will get up half an hour early,
String out – though it be but a humid, crop killing Wednesday –
A flag too large for its staff, damn near kill himself
Climbing the balustrade to fit it into
Clips poorly latched to the guttering.
I bet for all the size of the cloth he's not read Jefferson.
He's got a right: it's his history too. His boys' Saturdays
Are battles in my bushes, good and bad, the play
Clean enough, the reasoning rational for front yards.
We have to live on opposite sides of the same fence,
Speak cordially now and again. For him life is far more real
Two dimensionally, in a darkened room, in the mind of a child.
Between us, democracy is his way of getting even. How many
Of his kind it takes to make a tyranny I can't guess,
But one is too many to have about. It is all I can do
To keep from talking politics to him with the back of a hand.
I move so as not to be heard, not to have to hear the revisionist details.
I think of my family sleeping inside, my will to protect,
The dark nebula this man makes of his citizenship.
We are alike in the last of our method.

KEPLER'S DISCOVERY OF ELLIPTICAL ORBITS

That much for a meal
Undercooked and the spice last year's,
But the serving girl is not bad
And a slap causes her to leap
Over the bench, but smiling,
With a giggle that says *slap me*
Again and the lace of her bodice
Already undone and for the change in my pocket
No doubt a room could be rented with her in it,
Laughing and spicy and all the energy
Of a fresh horse whipped, and whip
I might. Whip, and she goes over
The table, her wonderful two-hands rear
In a plate of hash, dusted off with the backs
Of her fingers. A man might be pressed
To last an hour with her, or even
Three men: a woman who never winds down,
Water rushing from the mountains at flood,
Yesterday's bread crumbs in her hair and stew
On the last of her arms and nothing about her
Held firmly in place, but strong,
All the strength and the understanding of what
With a gentleman or any man or the boy
Taken by the inn to draw the water,
She could do, a citizen needing
Only a solid bed, good flooring,
Air in great bites and an earth
Immobile.

SELF-TAUGHT

Pass me the last section of the paper.
I'll have chance to read the headlines,
Scan a full article or so, before
I've got to step out on the porch again,
Run the sons-of-bitches off. I hear
In the mountains there's quite a plague,
The bastards are dying by the buckets,
Good people can't keep up with burying them all.
Here, the mosquitoes and still water,
Yellow fever has come back and runs garrulously
From house to house. I open the door,
Yell at the people nosing over our tomato plants,
Shout an obscenity you'd rather I preserve
At a man carrying away one of our
Purely ornamental shrubs. You'd have me
Let them take the whole damn garden away
And I might as well – it's most to gone.
You sit day and night in that chair, would not
For all the promises I could make in a week
Turn a cupful of soil. Cold on the way,
And starvation will set in, they'll be
Eating each other by first snow –
Would be eating us had I not the guns,
A son to keep watch while I sleep.
The good wife, the stable wife, I can't
Make you understand that soon the end of the world
Will not be made solely by angels drunken and
Shouting commands from the top of our house.

Come winter or spring, and we'll have
To fend for ourselves. You stay
Indoors, keep your fingers busy with innumerable,
Inconsequential acts. Outside, some idiot – bent
Boils and dysentery – dies square on our stoop
And though you'd rather I not I take a shovel
And put the squandered mass to earth.
On the roof, the angels laugh, point,
Tell me my turn is coming and the fire
In me like a metalsmith's I fling that shovel,
Get them to rise just a bit from the house,
Their brilliance shorted a moment to half as much.
For all their raiment, they perform like gulls.
Inside, a good shovel gone, I'm glad to see
You've moved about a bit, employed arms and legs,
Carried a garbage pot to the window, emptied it.

THE PLEASANT COUNTRY

As a child I liked
To use the knife. Sister drew back.
Mother turned her head. Father
Bent into my face, all
Hollow mouth and teeth,
And handed me the blade.
The sow was no true target.
Lowered to be within my reach
The animal, stunned by Father's
Proficiency with a bat, hung still
And I drove straight through the throat –
My fingers white flame at the knife handle,
Passing with metal, material following material.
Dark warmth spread across my arm,
The resistance needed to spur me.
I put my weight behind it
And Father said no no no

Slice.
Slice. Like this.
We'll hang another.
A slow motion, ear to ear,
Methodical. You will do better.

THE PRESUMPTION

Three antelope await the sunset.
A lion, hidden by the grass,
Smells the coming of darkness.
A gibbon clutches his tree
And fans the last of the light over him.
Coming across the field, the Salvation Army Band
Is making a mess of the day's end.
Before the trumpets elephants are racing,
Running towards the sparser grass,
Heading for scrub. Beneath dark shoes
Ants are being crushed, arachnids
Even as they try to gather the stray shatterings of light
Are smeared against soil. A jackal
Thinks to rush for the woman
Leading the cortege with her tambourine,
But it is growing ever darker, the trees
Growing ever more gaunt, the great herds of beasts
Ever farther away. Desert is being planned.
There is little to gain beyond honor in resistance.
Behind: the farmers, the farmers.

THE FIRST MURDER OF PONCE DE LEON

The shore stinks.
There is garbage on the ocean.
Rats chase each other in the reeds.
The path leads west.
Someone coming this way before
Left yellow arrows on the sides of oaks.
There are red marks on the pines.
Even out here you can hear
The bursting of water, waves
On stone masonry. The boys
Are stripping to their trunks.
Spray beats like diamond on our shields.
The sharks in the Fountain of Youth
Are tapping their noses against air.

WINNING THE LOTTERY

We find another one in the hills.
So far the disease has not spread
To livestock or humans, but I think
Soon enough at least wild game
Will come to nothing, the wood will be silent.
Weeks ago the first dead angel turned up
Out behind Simmons' barn, well along already
To decay – little more than a film over light,
A shade of serious blue. Shortly they were turning up everywhere:
Caught in clothesline wire, in gardens,
Glimmering on porch roofs. Two dozen corpses,
A few half-way fresh, and we knew it was a plague,
Could see the risings of shadows out of illumination.
Since then we've been worried to let them lie,
Worried to handle them enough to haul them away.
I've seen many a wasted angel I'd have rather
Let return to static brilliance than get sufficiently close
To put her onto the wagon, fold her wings
Shut and drop the fading body into earth.
Of late, though, we've seen more live ones –
Milling about pantry doors, stumbling ill
Through dog pens, turning to the heights
Just outside the Farley place and disappearing.
The most of us came together, decided
For the risk of contagion we couldn't let them collect,
Cough out so near their last few days – and so
We wind our way through these woods,
Expect at any moment to round a copse

And find them stretched, gasps of smoke,
Greater sickness than our carbolic can handle.
Every man has thought this hunt may be his last,
The buboes transfer from ethereal to corporeal,
In so broad a seminal power poor flesh
Be consumed with germ to the point
Of suddenly, sharply leaving still working bone.
We wouldn't allow a single atheist amongst us.

DEFIANCE

The caged violinist sings.
His wooden violin strict
In one corner of the cage
Leans against its bow, fracturing the spine.
At a table not far removed
Four dinner guests sit in silk,
A white tablecloth with silver tea service.
One man raises his ear to the voice;
The ladies present pull at their teacups.
The man in the most fortunate position
For observing the cage wonders
How strong the lock must be
To hold a seasoned musician.
The violinist places his hand over his heart,
Bursts into the highest note of the night.

BURNING HOSTAGES IN THE CHURCH

The object was to nail one shutter shut
Just well enough that, on the last try
It would swing open, and one person would get safely out.
You would make that shutter generally one at the rear,
And then set the front door afire. From there the conflagration
Might run so slowly that the troops would go home –
And cautiously, just seconds beyond when
Anyone might see, but before the skin
Gave in to flame, one girl would slide,
Glass minded and crying for breath, into snow. With tact
You could use ten gallons of gasoline, and still produce
A fire that took a life-granting time to get good hold.
The street side of the building in flame to the second story –
The back window would still wait for the right number
Of shoves, endure just long enough for there to be
No suspicion, for potential witnesses to be already thinking
Of the parasites breeding unchecked in their beds.
The girl would lie in the snow the lengthiest part of her life,
In the sound of her name forgetting the others,
Forgiving you in the love of exhaustion. Or it would be
A boy, an elderly lady, someone who years later
With a curious circular logic would want to run steel
Through your spine. Or no one would get out.
No one would try that back shutter often enough,
Or gather himself soon enough from the panic.
Stupidity, hysteria, lack of will
Killed as many each day as madness or malice.
You drove the nail less deep than you could have.
You are not to be blamed.

COMING OF AGE

The people of the situation comedies
Are your age. Their atrocities
Are not as noble as your own,
But you lack the laughter. Serious
To derision, their mistakes
Are ones you are too bright for.
And being too bright
You will not do well in rerun.

THE ACOLYTE

Fred's angel farm was doing damn well.
The book said a starter kit and six weeks
And half the crop would be ready for picking,
Most of the county would be at his door
Money in hand. It turned out well
For Fred. We thought it was a come-on,
A scheme designed just for men like Fred,
The ones who'd trust a Bible salesman
Whose female assistant wore satin pants.
Twenty-three dollars, plus another four in postage and handling,
And after two weeks a box the size of a television stand
Showed up at the post office, waited an hour
For the man who checked every day to pick it up.
I kept a watch for Fred to pop into the store,
Buy the usual six pack of beer he bought the times
He'd come up stumped, tell us all
Something went wrong. A month
And you could see the small things milling about
In the pen behind his barn. Fred was proud
To have anyone over, to stand leg propped
On a fence rail, that stupid, believer's smile,
As a guest poked wings, felt the arc of haloes,
Shook a head in disbelief. At the sale,
Twenty families bought one angel apiece,
Rushed the purchases home to find, eyes open,
They'd bought nothing but a dog, cat
Or six-day old pig. Morning, back
At Fred's place, each family carried an angel,

Felt gowns and compared glows, went home
To set loose pigs and cats and dogs in their living rooms.
Some made the trip a dozen times back and forth
Before finally turning their angel in, getting their money again.
Fred has put up a perch in his barn,
Has let the angels board there. He worries,
Winter coming, how to provide them all with heat.
The offer gave a money back guarantee,
But only if nothing grew. I think he is beginning to see
He's got good and stuck. Now and again
An angel will flutter away, get beyond Fred's property,
In mid-air change to dog or pig or cat,
Crash fatally through trees or field.
That way in a while the man will be free
From the burden of caring for them. Me,
Now I'd just turn them out in the woods,
Take the shotgun to those who refused to go.
Fred hoses the filth out of their pen,
Is seeing them these days as the lesson he hasn't hope to learn.

MACHINE INTELLIGENCE

These are the Absolutists.
They plug into the wall all at once.

These are the Constitutionalists.
They take their oil from the same can
Left to right.

These are the Anarchists.
They lie in rusty water,
Spouting senseless love lyrics.

These are the Communists.
They have spare parts.

These are the Nihilists.
They wrap themselves in flesh-tone prostheses
And lie curled like serious cats
In the satin sheets of human beds.

THE LAST MANIACAL STAND OF THE THEORETICAL
PHYSICISTS

The laws of supersymmetry provide eleven dimensions.
Even leaving gravity out, a unified theory
Gives us four dimensions, phosons
And the monopole. Sleptons would be,
In spring with the rains too heavy,
Too much. Not that anyone minds
A little decorative mathematics. Particles
That make up particles that make up particles,
That make up parts of specs in bits
Is all right, on the face of it. In a liberal nation,
Teflon coming out of the space race,
And cable TV as well, anyone can pass off
Big numbers as a way fancy folk
Might talk with God. Half of us believe in the big bang,
Or — at least in the rain
Cussing the dogs that get into our trash
And drag it half across creation –
Don't disbelieve. At some point, though,
A man is far enough behind. Protons
Decaying and neutrinos with mass
Are things you can nod your head about.
Three-symbol equations look easy.
But dimensions collapsing and sufficient heat
To make out of all the forces in the universe
God Himself – but only for fractions of a second –
Is more than a man with notables in his pants
Can put up with. I like the stars.

I find some good in gravity. The nuclear forces
Have a surcharge on my electric bill,
And I pay for the most part on time.
But the more a physicist sounds
Like a cheap-tent revival preacher, the more I watch
For his eyes on my wife, the more I ask
Doesn't he think I have smarts,
And what kind of hick does he take me for.

THE SURRENDER

The game is waiting at the edge of the field.
A squirrel perched like weed upon your fence
Looks to see what you will do next.
It is your ball game. He has given up.
So too the wolf, the moose, the jays,
A stray calf lost last week by the McClellan's.
You have won. The land is yours
And all things upon the land
Are you. Say what shall be done;
Make your order of everything.
The flesh and fur, blood and bones
Are tired of being the wild periphery of substance.
It is now up to you. You have at last
The right of definition.

THE END OF THE MUNCHKINS

The last scarecrow came from a farmhouse.
How long he had hidden in the closet
No one knows, but I suspect that
A century at least he had held his time.
He was content to send us from the garden;
Before him the last would have had a handful of us
Had not he started to come apart,
Had not the draw string about his pants given way.
We are getting few in number. Yesterday
Two of our people by a lion were eaten.
The dark is now the suspicion of eyes,
A feint of breath at the neck. Had I
The ruby slippers I would save my race,
But without the wish I cannot know how.
My own home by a tin man was beaten
To splinters. He used but the blunt end of his axe
And still the house came easily to pieces. Broom and all
Our earlier nemesis was a better lot; our cities
Stood, we held together to keep the roads intact.
I should rather be prey than only somewhat in the way.
The girl with her dog and legs like a blacksmith's
Has thought herself home and left us
The unmanageability of her johns' self-reliance.
Scarecrows, lions and woodsmen number more
Than we ever thought. A tin man
We've trapped in a pit at main-square and
A drop at the time I need find the limits of resolve.
We can be a people that lives of survival,

The quality of potatoes. I have no choice
But to think of fire, imagine rifles, teach
My countrymen what a substance water can be.

THE CONSERVATIVE SWEEP OF 1980

The old-timers are singing Dixie.
A black man sweeps the porch
Careful not to upset the singers' chairs:
Those squeaking, quarrelsome rockers.
Today Sam has a special on Nehi:
It is but a nickel again.
At the garage: Ron has his '49 Ford tuned
And fills it at the pump, cranking
The aged handle, letting gravity
Work for him. Soon
There will be a cloud of dust,
The road will be no more than his means.
Aunt Mary stands in the doorway
Draped in apron, her solid body
Alive with joy. The standard smell
Of home cooking draws conversation,
Ends the endless chorus of Dixie.
Presently, Jane – smooth, pleasant,
Certain the good husband, the appreciative glance –
Works her way to the back of the house:
Secure, unworried now of rape for all this sudden domination.
Rain begins at the tin roof, sulphuric acid
Falling about in furious puddles, splitting
The dust, agitating the discarded cans.
Acid rain steaming in anger
Patters even Jane's bedroom window,
Aunt Mary's kitchen exhaust pipe,
But who would wish to know it?

Dinner is ready. I have not seen
Such a spread in years: gray tubers,
Boiled wood, old papers torn into salad.
Prosperity is upon us. The whole if it
Tastes to me like steak, just like it;
Or veal,
The innocence still caged in the meat.

THE WITCH TRIAL

We can't keep a light bulb alive.
When she's been around one for three days,
Sometimes four, it will go suddenly out,
Burned black at the tip and the filament
Rattling. What type of light it is makes no difference.
I've lost one car headlight, the bulb
In the refrigerator, a light in the dining room,
The spot light from the back of the house.
She does nothing special, makes no attempts
To draw out the light, or dam it up,
Or use it more than a normal person approves.
But give her her way with light, and quickly
It is gone. Even the long-life bulbs,
The ones that cost too much even at the discount store,
Cannot stand up to her. I make no claim
Of knowing how it is done, or whether she tries,
Consciously or otherwise, to do it. I have
A half bag of spent bulbs. When the electric comes in
I hope to compare this month's bill with the last;
With weather and rate change one month might not tell much,
But if it goes on, in months a pattern might
Come out. The light in the hall
Has gone most recently. Now
I leave off all the light that isn't
Absolutely needed, and keep half a dozen bulbs
On hand, thinking those might last
Even her worst night. I give no thought
To mechanism. I pull the switch

And out comes light. I am not a rich man.
Nothing costs as little as it did
Just a year ago, or is as easy to find on sale.
She shrugs her shoulders and blames the workmanship.
The cost of bulbs is killing me.

THE PLACE IN THE DESERT WHERE LAST YEAR THE HORSES WERE EATEN

From beneath them, the world
Is quite a close place. Pressed against
The white bars the atmosphere tries
To get at you, but it cannot – and you
Hold your breath to thank the strength.
Looking down, they are but the sense
Of a failed machine. The ossification seems
Far more brittle than it can really be.
You worry why the whole of it is not more covered,
Why these ribs jut out so like a canopy.
The crime is that they last at all.
Gray stakes, gray fence posts,
Cudgels, corset, landmark – they can be
Anything but mere bone.
Personal need was never adequate reason.
Your stomach draws itself to the lungs,
But the system works. The kidneys
Press and the bladder fills. The walls
Of each vein hold. Above this fragile
Remainder you pound, a small stone
In your fist, beating
The memory out of this place
And your dry mouth tells you
How good it was.

THE GAME FIGHTS BACK

You do not know what to do.
Brown and yellow leaves part,
Branches wave up and down like flags.
A squirrel is rising on his rear legs
Perched as though porcelain on a stump.
Shotgun at your shoulder you make
The proscribed hesitation. A deer
Marches to the fence running east-west along the woods
And drapes his prize antlers over a post.
Two rabbits raze autumn debris
Out from the stifling shadow of oak, birch.
You move a hand from the trigger, counting
The tips of the shells in your pocket,
Mouthing the numbers out loud. Two bears
Step from the brush and lie unaware
In the grass not twenty yards before you.
You do not know what to do.
From behind you, tied to his cross,
The scarecrow screams *Fire, you damn fool!*
And you know it is he
For whom the gun aches, for whom
Your flesh has carried you all these years.
Again, *Fire you damn fool!*

THE DESTRUCTION OF THE HALF ANGELS

We let them do as they like
And often that leeway they carry too far.
Some with wings, some with only haloes,
They wear their gowns, or do not wear their gowns,
And we start to complain and then wonder
Who are we to criticize. Yet everyone knows
That Farley shacked up with a half-angel
For more than three months and came away
With no respect for them at all, said
She had an appetite that wouldn't quit, but a performance
That after two weeks did not fit the bill.
Parents worry of their children at dating age –
Half-angels with a great sense of absolute right
But no sense of justice or respect for the less perfect
Can get to be increasingly demanding: who could blame
A child for giving in – or even for, by the glory over carried,
Actively seeking to do more in one evening than normally
Proper. In a while the community's question will be how
Do we deal with the quarter-angels, and then
The octoroons. How small
An ancestry of angel will it take before
Responsible people feel a safe moral license
To turn a miscreant over the knee, or to box
A daughter's impatient lover. Every so often
A half-angel takes its wings and its half-feathers
And flies half an awe-inspiring distance,
And we swallow our practical considerations
A bit longer in praise and worship.

We remember how light and unbendable were
Their full-blooded parents, how much
Soaring there was. A half-angel is accused
Of murder or rape and the question becomes
How can we doubt, how dare we fix blame,
What blindness is it that allows us not to see
How propitious the half-angel's service was. The dissenters
Demur and stay to their own kind, but we have seen
Now and again a half-angel bleed, and it is only time
Before we believe once more that the best hope for our race
Is in curing our faults by ourselves. We go about our work
And sing praises when we are expected to, turn our eyes
When six half-angels have a go with the high-school English teacher.
Our tools are sharp, our hands not made for subtlety.
Some of us still respect a broad back and a man
Who lets his neighbors, whatever their mode
Of ecstasy or salvation, alone. Our questions
Will be put to rest, and all the more surely
For so humiliating a wait.

REALIZATION

The polar ice cap is melting.
Along the floor of the shopping center
You shuffle in knee-deep water. Packages
Of soup crackers, panty hose, overshoes
Float by, bumping your shins, diving
Along your ankles. Like snakes
Your feet move cautiously. Sweat
Pours from beneath your hair; sweat
Rolls down your arms, your stockings.
Peering through the tops of your glasses
You select from the shelves a handful of this,
A box of that, checking each from your intimate weekly list.
The damp bag lies nursing at your breast.
Slowly you wade past the cash register, through
A turnstile. The double doors inch open.
The water in the parking lot is maniacally sweeping into the street.
Cardboard skims by. Bottles
Leap along at three times walking pace.
Hastily rigged pontoon boats swirl at the curb.
Rafts drift past filled with howling drunks.
How ever to board with a sackful of groceries?

THE HANDS OF AN ANGRY GOD

I've stacked yet four again in the pantry,
Found room somehow for two more in the shed.
There isn't another slack of land to be
Taken up, a depth of soil to be
Overturned. The rocker for the press about it
Is no longer my resting place. The kitchen
Is a mess and I worry how you can keep
A routine: last nightfall the meal
Swam with bits and tatters of a soul I stacked
Weeks ago in one of the cabinets. The dog
Thursday tore one to shreds, battered it
Like a sock and that soul is gone.
Open the bedroom door
And we will be knee-deep in them.
My thought to make of many a balustrade,
To hold up the roof of the porch, perhaps
To stash even more atop it,
Failed in a shearing and collapse. They are
So insubstantial a commodity, not much,
Worth little time or use. I grow tired
Of having them fall out of the closets at me,
Of finding your fresh washed skirts
Draped across their shoulders.
Home can get damned cluttered when
Like cordwood they become responsibility.
I think to see another one unraveling
Will be the end of me: quiet as they are
They come between me and so much else.
And, though I love the old place, if ever
They come to, I am moving out.

THE CARNIVAL

The shadow of a dog falls for the moon.
On the road the cars that pass this night
Are counted, and for that seem more than ever before.
You want to know why I am walking the hall
And I tell you this county claims to have
More ghosts per capita than any other county
In the entire nation. I believe it could be so
As we have much land, with few people,
And our people harbor a meanness that
Through smiles and simple ways could last past death.
The windows open, I can hear their iron wolves
Hunting just down the road a mile, driving stakes
And stretching line in a field that for the work
Will be no better when they leave. We are
Too small a place for them. Families,
Occasionally the pack of boys emboldened with beer,
The one girl with a walk to stop traffic,
The poor end of a lane not quite long enough.
There is one stoplight and that blinks,
And no one here has killed a bear in three years.
In the dark I finger my fishing license,
Can feel my name. The Corn-Popper,
The Twister, dart throw, even burlesque.
You want me to want, I want me to have.
I'll sleep late in the morning,
Tomorrow all day be somebody else.

THE MAINTENANCE OF THE GIANTS

They sit with their hats on their knees.
They watch the door. A small woman
Busies about their feet, clearing away.
In tight collars and starched pants
They wait almost without moving, listening
As a man of no consequence, barely ankle high,
Talks about repairing hinges, about
Getting a ladder, about how,
With the door being so high,
Metal to metal and wood to wood
Will always make noise. He is not so angry
As happy with anger. His largest tools,
In matchbox beside, are the size
Of thumbs, accurate and without power.
The man to whom he speaks
Is a cough in dark tissue, worthless
In wind or rain. From deep
Within the next room a number is called,
So faintly all the giants lean near to the ground,
Looking to the door as though they could see noise.
In laps hats are bent and shirt sleeves sing.
One giant rises, looking carefully down
To see that the woman is nowhere near,
Embarrassed when the groan of his chair
Halts the garrulous repairmen. In steps
No longer than his own foot he shuffles after
The noise. The receptionist would rather
He had never come at all. He would rather

He had never come at all. He could lift
The roof with one arm. His huge hands gracefully
Kiss the edge of a tiny desk, fold
Almost flat on the carpet. He is saying
I am sorry.

THE POLITICAL INDEPENDENTS

I think the father would have done best
To let nature alone. Every time the boy
Reached out with the left hand the father
Growled, swatted it. The boy sat on his
Preferred hand at table, had to eat
With the right. No matter what fell on the floor,
Nor how long the boy took to feed himself,
The father waited, made sure the offending limb
Was kept down. Of late the family
Has taken to tying the arm back, to having the boy
For hours waddle about with the use
Of but one hand. He'll learn alright,
Be a gawky child, but put out the right.
His mother accedes because it is the father's wish.

Weekends I come up along the gatherings
Of the once left-handed men, catch them
Comparing right arms, popping biceps
That could lift small horses free of the ground –
The spindly, withered other dangling
From shirt sleeves like a continuation of cloth.
Half the night they'll be arm wrestling,
Single handedly pulling saplings up. And then
Some mostly drunk bastard will in absent-mindedness
Throw up the left, try to pull chest high a glass.
I watch from a safe distance the embarrassed men go home.

Every time that boy brings the left
Too quickly against an object that requires two hands

The father again beats hell out of him. I reach
For the lamp, extending my good left arm
And in straight line of sight from the bedroom
You wince. The father had once a fine left hand,
A powerful arm, put out that left appendage
As much as I, perhaps more.
And then he had a son.

THEOLOGICA MAGNIFICA

There were trees that reached into Heaven,
On whose uppermost limbs God sat
Spying like a ringmaster on His angels' simonies.
One mountain in each range
Rose past the Place of the Dead.
In large herds of every animal,
Guarded in the center, sat a ghost-beast,
One animal-god that could control the grass,
The rains, winds and hearts of predators.
This was so. The lightning fell in our midst
Like the corpses of lost game
And we clamored around the name of our God.

But this came to nothing; Heaven
Came and lay upon us, smothering
Our small souls with unwanted brightness
And we pulled fire out of the stricken tree
And made its lightning set flame to God's beard
And then we stood, but only on hind legs
And counted the stars
And Heaven leaped back in fear
So far, so far, so far.

THE CHANGELING

Three feet tall, my arms are lost
In the shirt, my legs somewhere
Under the bunched pants, my feet
Still, at my age, in a child's sneakers.
I smoke and cuss like a sailor,
Am much beloved at every tavern in town for my antics.
Deep in the woods the child whose name I inherited
Now hunches on all four, has learned
To be gentle, to hold back his giant's strength.
What my natural parents wanted with him
I haven't the damnedest idea. But he must
Be worth a great deal, for my adopted parents
Cried, tore the rugs, screamed, scouted
The forest and almost boiled me alive
When their suspicions finally gave over
To certainty. They could never love me
Until, when school age, human children teased this elfling so greatly
They had in defense to accept me. Short,
Stubby, capable of wiggling my nose,
Wrinkling my skin, I did all I could to please them;
But always there was the other. I imagined him
Growing first as large as the kitchen table,
Then the size of the couch. Eventually,
All the doors would be altered, and that
Wouldn't last. A few years and his place
Would be out back, little more than a stall,
His clothes handmade and mostly rags,
Nothing unbreakable anywhere around.

I dance on a midshipman's table
And the three drunks stuff dollars in each
Of my huge, sagging pockets. My little, scratchy
Voice howls out songs for whores and onanists;
I put my whole head in a pitcher of beer.
The huge bastard, turned out, taking care of himself,
Hard to fit and feed, I can see
Spending weeks alone by a stream in the deep forest.
I make faces at a man with a red beard,
Run in hiding beneath a serving girl's skirt,
Pick coins from the floor, smell new sounds,
And my fear is in a monstrous child
Somehow finding Home.

VICTORY CELEBRATION

The military like wheat come home.
Fathers are not themselves. Mothers count
Fingers, toes, eyes, dark patches of skin.
Sisters dance fertility circles while brothers
Search soldiers' pockets for lost ears,
Loose testicles, a souvenir envelope
Stuffed with enemy hair. All the whores
Do anything for free. Drinks to uniforms
Are on the house. Pregnant wives
Are hiding in stiff closets. Alas,
Gonorrhea is everywhere and everyone
Wants a case. Huge flags
Are flung into obscure weather. Speeches,
Addresses, telephone numbers, meetings
Beneath the bleachers, behind the bushes.
Twelve naked men and the sophomore homecoming
Queen dance courtship geometry on the roof. Boy,
This is some party. Please
Pass me another bowel of the dead.

THE PROBABLIST

There is nothing the wood will not give
If you work it long enough.
I have taken this piece from the best tree,
Felt the life shudder out of it through
My axe. The chisel now
Will give it life again. Surgeon,
I bring out the face and hands,
The heart and eyes and breast.
In the dark collar of cellulose my wife
Waits for my power to bring her
Light. Axe and chisel,
Razor, I beat the yellow rings,
Strip to perfect depth the bark.
Patience is the length of a man. I am
That which makes all that I own
Mine. You shall be
What I have thought of the privacy of wood.
You must be the warm house, the adequate table.
A thigh a waist a desire a bray.
The tree comes away from you and we
Are almost one. See me!
This tyranny will not be the last.

LEARNING THE SURVIVAL STRATEGY

The boys step delicately over warm puddles.
Fallen leaves along the tractor ruts rise in anaerobic swirls.
Patches of sun, like water through the roof,
Patter on ridiculous blotches of grass straining
In the once lean, hard path. Two hundred paces more
And the clapboard barn juts out of the land:
Ivy and rotten board, broken machinery,
The skull of a horse. Someone's older sister
May wait for a boy with hands like mice,
A mouth like wax. Men and women
May dance harvest paganism, wandering afterwards unquestioningly away
In hopeful twos through the forest. Water pooled inside the barn
Rustles with bare feet, imagined cloth,
Insubstantial silk, the dreams of razor thighs.
Boys with their rubber mallets, their plastic arrows,
Their long feathers, mud paint and loose skin costumes,
Rush the door, voices pressed into the dark like pikes.
Around and around in the straw, in the loft –
Hypothesized blood, teeth garnishing the pounded dust floor.
In the corner of vision a fading blonde hair;
Unholy, innocent breaths trailing to the last dark convex
Where perhaps broad blue eyes half-eagerly await
Avenging counter-savageries. But not death.
Not death.

THE DIVINITY STUDENT

There's a man on the corner selling rabbits.
He has them tied to the edges of his kiosk.
They dangle by their hind legs and those
Nearest the wheels he had to set
High on the wagon when he moved, so the product
Would not snare in the spokes. Fresh game
Is so rare. At the front of the cart
The rabbits are gutted and drained; at the back
Their bellies are yet warm. He wears
A rabbit fur coat, rabbit fur shoes, rabbit cap.
His belt is cartridge casings. Father asks him
Where he gets so many, and the man
Recounts crossing the land just north of Pamlico,
Running along the water – no dog, no bait –
His rifle set in an arm bent to a V,
The long shot clipping two in line. With my thumbs
I push the hard knot of a stomach across fur,
From the base of the ribcage to the crotch.
Mother wants something that already is clean.
Nights the man has let me into his barn,
Has opened the cage doors, let the animals
Move in their short locomotions across free straw.
A boy can hold one or more to his ears,
Listen to the blood beneath warmth,
The spooling enzymes, peristalsis,
The feed becoming rabbit.
I think he lets all the children at one time or another
Squirrel down in the floor of the barn with his stock.

When he rolls in his cart, washes the wheels,
Spreads the accumulated tethers on a table,
I stand as close as I can, smell in the air
The gray carbolic he uses, watch
The rabbits' noses twitch, notice he wears
Rubber boots.

PUBLIC EXECUTION

He is ready.
The lights go dim,
The room blinks,
And nothing.
Strapped in his chair
He starts, expectant.
Again the switch is hung
And pulled.
The lights go dim,
The room blinks,
The audience bends forward for carboned air,
And nothing.
The show is stopped.
A man wearing gray headphones
Advances to check the wires,
To run his small hand tenderly about the plugs.
He tugs the straps,
Rattles the prisoner's headpiece.
He asks the man to raise his arm
And apologizes for the inconvenience.
Once more, all is ready.
The man in the gray headphones
Pats the man in the chair
And explains difficulties.
The switch again is hung
And pulled.
Blue invades the reposed man's body.
Eyes pound glaucous at the ends of their sockets.

Sparks find home in hair.
Even with safe, efficient electricity,
There is always a smell of burning.
Finally, the circuit adequately complete,
The man relaxes against death.
Milk thick eyes refuse to reclaim their frames.
All is accomplishment.
The man in the gray headphones
Counts by his watch
And signals videotape. A boy
Proud to be an integral part
Cues the guards. Dinner is served.
Housewives in aprons do not look as good as they should.
Pass the potatoes. Don't play with your corn
So. You've forgotten your manners.

MAKING THE MISTAKE

The dead get up and walk.
Cemeteries burst like clusters of peonies,
The deceased remove what they can
Of their former selves, tentatively
Begin the reintroduction to motion.
A few come out of basements, step
Out of closets, form in mid-air,
Walk out of the sea as though it should cause
No notice at all. People near the miracle
At first lock themselves in second story bedrooms,
Have impressions from a thousand horror films,
Can feel fingers with the flesh falling off
Reaching for their throats, or fondling their breasts.
Some run out into the street nervously singing,
Falling in front of the moving dead with clasped hands.
The dead move around them, occasionally
Brush a shoulder – or stop, being blocked
By a family with all eyes forced shut.
After a while, people unlock their doors,
Come down to the first floor, grow tired
Of kneeling in good clothes against gravel.
Young couples begin to stand in front yards,
Watching the dead mill aimlessly about, making open speculation
About the dead in other states, in other countries.
We stay by the living room window,
Our legs in the couch, trying to get the courage
To go outside and sit on the porch,
To wave and see if one will wave back.
Behind, in the kitchen, our children
Are painting themselves, stripping to underwear.

THE REPATRIATED PHYSICIST

I start down the road, going to get him
One more time. I'd let him stay,
Be done with him: but that he's your son
I'm sure, and for you I'll go after him.
You put a lantern on the porch,
Took out bread for when we come in.
He's in a public house again, squirrelled
To a knot by the fire, leaning over
The table to bluff ordinary farmhands
To believing in imaginary numbers,
Discoursing loudly on chemistry, coming damn close
To heresy in spouting physics. For good measure
I carry the rifle: the innkeeper may have
An unliberal constitution, a yokel
May think he is being made fool of.
Two strong arms are not now enough
To pull the boy out of the holes he digs for himself.
His fingers as stiff as calipers he'll wrestle
Some red-gartered bar flop into a corner,
Be pressing her with Doppler effects,
Having her resort to modesty in the face
Of his electron shells, spurious entropy.
I put on the coat of a bear I killed
And skinned myself, set stupidly out. The blue-shifted child,
His vision a tunnel with objects
Recently passed yet cluttered at sight's edge,
The coming space an extenuated chromatics,
Will see me stretched or squat,

An instant or a millennium, transmogrified
By our relational speeds – and hide
Behind some day laborer's pockets. He knows
There is yet a crop to get in, honest dirt
To fit beneath fingernails, his mother's
Half luminous pantry theories of nutrition.
All along the street as I pass
Sharecroppers put out their lights, close curtains,
Lock doors. They understand that coming back
I'll travel twice as fast as ever the boy could.

COMING TO REASON

This should not happen in a city this size.
Angels forgetting how to fly,
To be beyond simple gravity,
Are falling to pavement. Not ten minutes
Ago I ran into one, bounced
The blood, halo, wings and gown
Across my hood. The moment I hit her
I knew she was dead. At the closest phone
I could not think of what to report,
The offense. Another was broken
Near the phone booth, a lump
Of radiant matter, a busted glow.
Some are yet living and there is nothing
Anyone seems able to do. On one roof
I saw one trying to stand, to collect
Its broken pieces and go on, but
Mechanics function alone for only so long and the beast
Gave up. Not more than a dozen yards away from me
A boy is dragging by the heel an angel's body
Toward the door of a gutted house,
And a man with spittle on his chin
Is bashing out the brains of an angel
Broken almost beyond identity: a mercy.
I think I could go and get my gun,
Could put the still living few quickly
Out of the suffering. I begin for my car,
My feet lifting off the pavement, the clutter
Below growing smaller, my clothes and limbs unaware
Of the massive nature of my person, the tops of buildings
Rushing towards me and the clouds but breath.

THE NATURE OF HOPE

Long about noon ordinary people begin waiting.
Families stand on porches, the father
Stepping out to the first porch step,
Looking beyond the edge of the roof –
His body yet under the eaves, but a neck
Bent into open air. Some stand in back yards,
Or gaze, while bent over kitchen sinks, through windows.
A man or two goes out to his fields,
Holds with the crop dry as leather
Crouched at his knees. Too late for one yield,
Too early for another. Men at the garage
Stop work, drink coke while watching the gray.
With the first whip of wind we see the drought chased out.
A minute or two and drops the size of quarters
Ricochet off barn roofs, splatter dust from panes.
Those who would have kept out to praise the water
Run for cover, stare from a crack of a back door.
Sober men think such a rain will too easily run off,
The ground one inch down remain brick.
But not a few are thinking of how a moment before
The sun was so perfectly round, so angry an orange,
So gutter-drunk pure. An hour
And the shower is done, the water is steaming up,
Growing land is harder than state road.
One man bends to the muddy puddle
Left at the end of a rain spout, touches a finger
To the muck, and then to his lips,
Says the water tastes as though it should have fallen

Far north. You can hear a man beating his wife,
Saying that it is her spells and incantations –
She shouting that it is his lost control
In sitting at nights too long with his own daughter.
Dogs stay at the far ends of barns and sheds.
The man with the water on his lips is saying
Far, far north. It is a good sign.

THE RESPONSIBILITY

Out back the boy is flogging a cow.
Something should be done.
Already the flies are eager for blood.
The boy grows wild for the sound
Of the beast understanding its pain.
If he is not stopped soon
There will be no halting him.
The cow has given no milk;
Try as we might, she is dry.

Father has made it to the porch
With his shotgun. In his house
There will be order, a procedure
For even the most mundane, the most
Absurd of things. From the painted,
Polished boards he calls to the boy.

The boy continues. Blood gathers on the ground
In Bolshevik puddles. Father calls again,
The boys arm in preparation flies ever higher,
The whip sings ever more maiden-like in its arc.
The cow raises her back to the blow.

Strained to the joy of his muscle

Father aims the gun, nudges the trigger.

His shoulder quivers eagerly with report.

Certain, carefully

The cow falls to its side. Here:

Leather, kidney, heart, lungs,

Stomach, the boy's unquestioning stare.

Order again.

THE SAINT CUTTING HER FINGER

First impulse: to go on.
The red drops
Let out the great under-skin electric,
The tension that not even
With the edge of a wire brush
Is scrubbed out.
It has been waiting
To slip out like a balloon's air
And the opportunity was quick,
Accidental. The body panics
To fortify its breach.
The blood begins to pile up,
To stop in an ugly coagulation
Like a wart at the finger's end.
Now an angle cut, proximal,
Would guarantee a promising stream,
The amperage would fall back
Becoming a small light at the back of the hand
Manageable in theology.

Kitchen mandrel, an application of salt.

MORAL SELECTION

You think you've seen the boy
Staring at you from the rafters of the barn.
With a dozen acquaintances you have spun
In the straw cleared of manure,
Your dress fanning tastefully in your twists.
The music has flung you about male arms,
Damp breaths have turned you this way and that
Like a stone. The noise you make on the floor
Is theirs as well as yours. You pass
From boy to expectant boy like heritage, certain
Of the eyes in the loft awaiting you,
The boy of the shadow – until
He is in front of you, holding out his arm,
Surprising you with candor. You spin
As though with anyone else,
Working towards the door, breathing his breath.
He should have waited:
Crouched in the forest, panting in one black corner
Of the barn, leaping to your screams like flame.
His darkness falls about your flesh like hope.
Here he turns you smiling at the tip of his hand,
Clutching you, forcing you of free will to give in.
You plead:
Wait in an unknown place, an unexpected time,
Steal back your identity.
Make of your hands claws.

THE INTERFACE

Every night he is out in the dark,
Hands above his head. He is able to do it only
For half a second or so. I'd never have thought
He could do it at all – would say he simply discovered
The phenomenon and made as though he caused it –
Were it not for the sweat I mop from him,
The smell about his clothes. I tell him
Our strength is in the hive, that what he does
If it does no good is no good. He goes out
Night after night, for the breadth of a few milliseconds
Holds the stars in place. Half my dark morning
Will be put into rubbing the red, strained
Muscles of a suddenly unknown man, soaking his clothes
In the tub. He is proud that he can hold the heavens
Fixed half an instant. But I think all that he does
Is cheat the world out of a nameless second's turning,
Press a little further the limits of what hell can be like.

GRANDFATHER

The grass has started to work itself backwards.
A blade is no more than a bit in the mass
And I am sure there is meaning to it.
Individually and in rows the life retreats.
I call the family: wife, two children,
Grandchildren, in-laws; they watch
And the grass pulls easily beneath earth.
The youngest among us stretch and wish
To race into the yard, to see closer the green
Slither beneath dirt. I will not let them
And it is my house, my yard, my grass.
Already, a bird by a clump of dandelion
Is drawn to ground level and sucked under.
The wife is pointing and laughing; a young father
Remarks what a feat it is for mere turf;
A small girl cranes to see the last of a wing go down.
I can feel the house shake, the subtle rumble of the porch,
And it is not soon enough, not soon enough.

FRANKENSTEIN

Ignorant lightning. The castle on the promontory.

An eager assistant. The mad doctor

Leering over senseless yards of tubes

Wires and rods, angered with the ephemeral.

The professor warns you not to believe.

But already the electricity is at your fingertips,

The world is at the edge of your eye.

The restraints will fail, the doctor will make his slip.

Even now you can hate the grinning assistant,

His hands in front of your idiot fact,

His palms blasphemous with fire.

THE COVENANT

Day after day it is the same,
Week on week, months on end.
I rely on it. You get a little
Mouthy, the neighbors again
Have all the cousins, uncles, aunts and
In-laws in the backyard for hamburgers
And beer, and I go out to the stoop,
Take three balls, spin them. More often
Than not, I drop a few. Time and time and time
They bounce, fly and fall. I feel
Gravity in my hands like life itself,
Watch at apex the nonliving material
Give in to physical urge, start the fall.
You stare out the window and yell
That I should not get so upset.
It may be selfish that when matters go awry
I list to the simple, expect gravity –
Use it to keep myself firmly seated.
From the porch I fling sticks,
Toss boards, hard rubber balls.
One evening I throw a small globe upwards
And, at what should be the end of its rise,
It goes on, draws to a small point,
Disappears as though happy to do it. Two more balls
I throw, each going the way of the first. A book.
Firewood. Newspapers. A lamp. The dog,
Howling in midair above the house,
Drifting upwards to a half whine, and then

Nothing. From the kitchen window
You mock me as our lawn furniture
Bowls through a cloud, grows
Too small to be traced. With the elements
And myself there is a mutual alliance,
Faith. Tonight, your idiot laughter
Still in my ears, your heavy sleeping form
In my arms like flour, I'll be running over
My contract – not entirely with gravity
Itself, but with its consistency. My biceps
Will ache and, bending the knees,
I'll make one huge toss. Midway
The morning I'll still be holding out my arms
To catch you just in case. But, wife,
I'll never be the same if you fall.

THE SUPPLICANT

Most of the innocuous remedies we tried first.
Everyone put on their best, went
To the only church that would hold the whole town
Congregated, and sang. Even the two or so
Town drunks — propped by the door, not entirely
In control of the words — wailed with us,
Stretched out in pleading. No use, the next month
The whole damn town, Sunday clothes,
Prostrated itself in the street – laid down
In the mud, the trash and animal droppings.
It did nothing. Full moon and the house
Still standing farthest from town center caught fire,
Whipped up like a single match, was gone in seconds.
The seasons of the moon well known, two days before
The family had moved their furniture
To a neighbor's shed,
Left for the flame only a shell. We built an altar,
Let a minister of each organized denomination
Sacrifice one of the stray dogs so common hereabouts.
Later we had the doctor closely inspect a school girl,
Sent her out in her mother's far
Too large wedding gown
To wait in the house that was to be next.
The bones we assume you can find in the ash,
But no one has gone to look. It is only a year
Before the business district is in line,
Less than a decade before town square itself
Will be next in the path. In months

We'll fall to human sacrifices, start on
Celtic rites. On the cinders of the first house to go
The Smiths have rebuilt, made a solid home,
Put in fewer flammables, heavier furniture.
Month after month the new house sits out there,
So far from the nearest yet unburnt place
That all you can see of it
Is the light from the windows.
This month we are dancing naked in a huge circle,
Shouting euphoria and praise for good fortunes,
And the Smiths stay home. It is but a while
Before we come together with the torch, show up
In that reseeded front yard, to put an end to their distance.
Mr. Smith looks from his door to the distant,
Still dim town center
Where we dance, where our banshee howls
Thunder along rooftops.
He waves the smoke from his fingertips,
Smells of the smolder of his children
Playing in the kitchen,
Calls in his wife from where she stands
Steaming outside in the mist.

COMING TO THE TRUTH OF SNOW WHITE

Out in the snow four birds
Converge on the issue of a footprint.
Not much of a footprint. Just a matter
Of crushed snow and water.
Unmistakably, however, it is a footprint.
A small, subordinate starling
Hops into the trench,
Pulling at the flat
Green leaves of barely visible grass.

Inside, behind the fog of the glass,
With his nose pressed to the pane,
One of the seven dwarfs
Peers out at the delicious looking bird,
Thinking: this new, fragile lady
Has such huge feet.

THE HAPPINESS

You'd like it all to be
Square roots and cosines,
Equivalent angles, ellipses,
Circles defined by Cartesian coordinates
And generated by quadratic equations.
It should be enough in one man's life
To prove the theory of limits
And we agree on this one thing.
In your room you'd have
The whole of the planet cut
To intersections of lines that don't
Really exist, but that we manage
For convenience to manufacture
And fix everything perfectly with.
Your mother and I for quite some time
Have thought it a good thing.
Your library is healthier than our pantry.
We buy pencils and paper and are lost
In parallelograms, trapezoids, tesseracts.
Fifteen, and you send the boys away.
McClellan's girl already looks like a whore,
Has me worrying about myself way past midnight.
Bib overalls or dress, for you it is the same:
The lattices between molecules, the strong
And weak nuclear forces, the angles of bondage.
We sit in the living room aware that
In three weeks you'll come to sixteen.
Of late we've heard you shuffling in the room,

Rolling the names of numbers on your tongue
As though in themselves they were substance.
Outside, all the small things you've wanted to believe
Are massing on the stoop. Soon I'll open the screen,
Point to the stairs, the slash of light under your door.
The rabble flooding past, too late
I'll see the imaginary numbers, the exact lines,
And swallow my hope of finding you, the neighbors'
Boys, the back of a van. All the approaching year
I'll have your mother teaching you the practical.

AT THE PROPER TIME

Some trees hold their snow.
Others let it drag into icicles,
Then rip and lie in small crystal puddles.
Five wolves chase the tracks
Of one rabbit. You hold your rifle
Like a candle stick. Out in the drifts
The wind makes snowmen, little helmeted
Bastards, who last a second and then
Leap into the white heap's lee. Your deer
Have passed to the North. The wolves are proof.
A hot bath waits; the cabin's dining room fire
Will blare like a devil's mouth. One shell
Is in the chamber, four in the stock.
The snowmen rise like Yeti warriors
And your shoulder aches for something to withstand.

Meanwhile, the sun is dying.
Your wife's leather skin arches along her back,
The claws of her feet dig in hardwood floors.
A boy watches at the window for Father
To bring home the corpse of anything. He has made
A wonderful snowman, the Komodo.

FAMILY REUNION

The bears have come-to for summer
Again. They shake their bandit thick hides
And settle into day, complacent.
A boy still outrigged in snowshoes,
I skip through the garden of a lady
Who wants the skin of animals around her.
She won't have my skin.
The old, rough-sawn bears would not allow it.
Their grunts and moans
Already fill the cultivated fields
And my small garden adventures,
Pictures of imitation, demand their protection.
They think I emulate bears.

They've yet to feel the winter in my shoes.

1930: SUBSISTENCE

The road descends to a point and always
It is a distance. Dust clouds rise
At the intersection hundreds of yards away
And another car is passing. The lane
Is for going down. No one
Travels the short way to this house.
We have many attractions.
And good structure can be put to good use.
I sit all night naked on the porch
Without fear of hellfire. The windows
Are open. A fox has been at
The chickens and it is nothing
To take the rifle and fire at a noise.
Freedom is the opportunity.
My overnight bag ages by the door.
I want to show my legs at a bar-and-grill.
I want to wink and know what I am doing.
I want to see if I can be
As good as the hogs. The screen door
Beats in the wind and father attempts
To adjust the spring. Metal object –
The man works its limits into it. Tight
Across my stomach it stretches
And my sweat must come to more
Than it is now. I go only so far.

INITIATIVE

There are different stars over Moscow.
The night is darker and the moon
Does not know just how to come up.
The physics are the same: there is still
Life in gravity. But birds fly at night.
In the city cats walk only on the sidewalk.
Ordinary men live their lives as a man
Living life by feel alone, deaf-dumb touch
Honed to a black line laid down in darkness.
There are no meteors, no comets.
The violence of the snow is usual.
People do not love their children;
They have them as though having
Gallstones removed. No one
Studies women, studies a girl
Half-grown but with all the signs
To raise wonder in good blood. Trees
Boil in the wind, but the wind
Goes nowhere: it changes in direction
As if with one mind, with a love
Of line and right angles. Light
Does not go far there. At night
People do not use their bathrooms.
Students five days a week
Know what they should. Children cry
By a law that no one understands
But whose pattern has become ingrained.
Husbands and wives touch as though

Through water at great depths.
When a dog barks it makes sense.
The blackness sucks up everything and no one
Cares, nor sees, nor would care to see
Stars or moon or blackness. Rivers awhile
Flow backwards. At midnight
Of newly born twins one is drowned. Crate packers
Eat little girls and the bones dance in joy.
The moon stumbles about, parting clouds
With one arm drunk and one arm sober.
Stars sputter, and more glower anew.

They are not our stars. It is not our moon.

OCCUPATION

Hawks buckle under the tremendous air pressure.
Along the shore, young girls are waving
As their fiancées packed in boats like fish
Are rounding the cape, setting off for unknown
Hostile lands. Inland, enemy soldiers eat gull.
Thousands of belligerent legionnaires line before the wagon
Of the carnival whores. Still the girls
Are offering men in uniform a discount.
Farmers, cautious this close to the war zone,
Are loading battle dead onto their wagons
Ready to plant the ragged flesh and hollowed bones
In muddy fields now infertile. Outside
The main thrusts of both armies,
Boys idled by the closing of the schools
Even now rape a woman and her two daughters.
Life goes on. We are sick to death
With the Conqueror's propaganda, but are doing well:
Full bellied, but humiliated with lines for fresh meat.
Pray these demons leave us in one piece;
Send silk stockings.

THE CHALLENGE

He starts early of a morning,
Walks past the Paterson place, past
The Post Office, Gunter's store, passes
The George garage, and most like by noon
He's out to the McClellan place.
What worries us most is he may
For months have been taking his morning walk –
Seen by many of us, waved to, treated
Like any other somebody no one knows.
What looks like dress slacks, gum-soled shoes,
Shirt and that brisk step. Webber
Brought it up, told a bar full of us
He'd seen the man the last four days running
Walking on the right side of the road, each day
As though in the footsteps from the day before,
A measured but swift pace. Next morning
Four of us got together, sat on the courthouse lawn,
Watched him come down the road, wave back to us,
Go on. None of us knows the son-of-a-bitch. Seems
He just showed up, walks, and is seen nowhere else.
He's got to eat, got to sleep, belong somewhere;
Probably has a wife, family. A week ago
I walked behind him a mile or more, got winded,
Will be damned if I'll spend the gas
To drive the car after him. What was once
A coven with knowledge of the man is now
The whole community: mornings lawns and porches
Are slick with families watching the man, waving.

His arm must get sinful tired.
I once tried to talk to him, got a good look
At his face, came away with only his smile.
The town is aflame to see him, is infatuated.
This odd interest will soon turn to question:
The novelty becoming puzzlement over where he goes,
How he comes back, where he starts.
People will glance out of windows as he passes,
Hold their breath, leave curtains closed until he is gone.
Drunken teenagers will boast of thinking to stop him,
Demand an explanation, hold him still
Until the whole story falls out. How many
Months, years, decades he has been amongst us
And walked unnoticed I can't guess.
But there are many of us here can see
We are letting our fear make fools of us
And we can't stand to be fools for long.
If you want to see him, you'd better come quick.
I'd bet the bastard doesn't even leave footprints.

ULTIMATE RESPONSIBILITY

Surely, one day I will have enough.
Long years I have not been able
To get into the house for the mass.
With ladder I poke more through
A second-story window and sleep
On the porch. I try never to refuse a gift
But many escape me. Just the other day,
The wind a terror, I ran a half-mile
To the ditch at the edge of the highway
And could gather but a handful of leaves
Before they crossed over. By the house
More were about the ground and there
I began again. Even in summer
I have a day's work. Rainstorms
Are a godsend. I need admit
Often I will not get them all,
But such brings me to more – to struggling
To pick faster, to climb the ladder quicker,
To push them through the window and start
Down with one motion. Each day
I am achieving more. I am doing better.
Certainly I am a fine thing in the eyes of my Creator.
One day I will have enough.

THE SMALL GODS

I take the broom and there is
Another one. His feet pound across dust,
Trip at the steps and he is under the house,
Two eyes damn blue and darkness.
The wife has one by the ears
And he is no weight: she holds him
At arm's length and goes to fling him
Into the garden. One jumps the fence
And runs for the woods. I've not checked
The closets but there are several under the bed,
A few in the bathtub, who knows
How many in the attic. The first time this winter
We lit the fireplace a handful of them in the chimney
Coughed the smoke back at us; one
More magical than most dematerialized
And came-to on the mantle, a sooty mess.
It does me no good to be making love,
All effort astride the wife, and see on the bedposts
A number of them as raptured as young girls.
The contract has gotten out of hand. They are
Too great a company for one house, garden and yard.
I would keep a few if I could trust them
To stay out of the way, but I see them now
In boiling pots, in the face of our meat.
We will run the majority out, but those
Hard to leave we'll put on the fire like logs:
Much brilliance and sizzle but little heat.
The wife has three caught in her skirts

And for the noise a man needs stop his ears.
Deaf between two palms I stand to the side
And the cloth about her body billows like hail.

THE LAST DAY

It has some improvement over ordinary rain.
Color for one. Yellow and blue. An occasional red.
Very little of that gray. And though I wouldn't want to be
Outside in it, there's something to its splatter and hiss
As it hits a cold surface. As long
As it doesn't burn through the roof
It will be pleasant enough. Next door
The young housewife manages to put on
A winter coat and ski mask, a pair of gloves,
And get clothes in from her line.
All the sheets already have holes, and no one tonight
Is going to dress. I haven't even run out
To put up the windows on the Ford.
An hour and you'll be home,
Hysterical, the car sputtering dead as it makes the driveway
From all the acid in the air. Thank God
You keep an umbrella. It will be eaten
To a fistful of flags by the time you reach the porch,
But you will have only a raw spot or two on your legs,
A set of ruined clothes, a burn on your cheek.
I understand some of the Baptists already have been out
Dancing in the pestilence, praising God and melting
To lumps of undistinguished flesh. This atmospheric deviance
Is going to bring out the worst in people.
Luckily the phone lines are down, and our door
On a bad side of the house for neighbors to run to;
Save the fact, I'd be inundated with apocalyptic visions,
Good people ready to take their medicine, crazed sportsmen

Wondering what this will do to the duck season.
My poor end of all this will be calming you down,
Running my hand along your shivering thigh and finding
If I can flatten your nerves enough to get fed
A little supper. The windows bubbling,
The roof beginning to run like a syrup and the front yard
A slush the bones of the car slowly sink into,
I'll sit back after dinner, think hard
About chasing you once though the kitchen,
Cornering you in the bedroom. Half the neighborhood
Is unbreathable gas, and here you are at the driveway,
A flash and two wheels into the last of the hedge.
Your face is unspotted, thoughtless terror and I can tell
Getting supper will be work enough for this one night.

THE MESSIAH

He could only see the tall men.
Only tall men existed, were considered,
Collected for community tasks. The family
Weddings, funerals, cookouts, he would invite
Simply the tall men – not, in particular,
Slighting the short ones, but refusing
To believe in them as they were under
Six foot. Pushing a car,
Mending fences, he would count
Only the tall men that showed to help.
Women, of course, could be any size.
His first son, five foot nine,
Came and went without recognition,
Was fed at the table by his mother,
Slept in the spare room, was never mentioned.
In a few years every tall man in the county
He knew by name. Trouble I expected, and, middling tall,
A third of the near populace stands now
At the swing gate – and he can't see
A one of them. Five foot six to five eleven
They grumble with the anger alcohol brings
To insignificant matters. I wait
Towering on the porch over the whole lot,
My five foot one frame strewing shadow
Across the forward half of them. No one
Near my stature can be seen in the crowd
And defending the man I feel the idiotic,
Desperate hope of those oppressed

By the grand who, in other circumstances,
Would be oppressed by the common.
He eats his meal by the open dining room window,
Hears nothing of the mass nor my arguments.
Some five eleven and three quarters bastard
Is sneaking through the back, will do him in
With a serving fork. The endangered man moves
As slowly as solar exhaustion; but his absolutist
Policies I begin to see as correct, to understand
This damned canaille may need his balance.
Eat, oblivious to the murderer padding
With unnecessary quiet in the pantry.
I'm telling the men from the porch
My dreams of being six foot four,
My experiments with standing on the second
Rung of a ladder, my stacking boxes together.

ETHICS

The last of it we won't see for years.
They've been hiding in caves, holed up
In attics, surviving in the trunks of cars.
In cases entire nations have given them refuge
And we have marched there. The mist-like bodies
Drawn naked and mounted on rocks we leave.
A few we put to the fire. A half dozen
Raped and bloody messes we've put into bags
And bounced to shatters of bone. Many an angel
I have broken the back of with my own
Hands. Our land is solid soil. The boy
Has learned what worth there is to the neighbor's daughter.
I'll not have the tables turned. We drag them
Out in the open, tear the haloes and robes,
Sport with the glands and sex, expose.
Arms bearing sudden bulk, broken backed angels
Try to pull themselves out of public spectacle.
Whole communities gather, watch the shimmering beasts
Expire into light. It's not what I enjoy,
But it's a practical matter.

THE SEAMSTRESS

The indecent goo slides evangelically out of the oven.
Holding her spoon at arm's length, Mother
Skims a bit of the crusting surface
And offers puffed lips tastes.
More spice, a half cup wood, two measures
Sod, a handful of freshly ground glass.
It must bake another hour.
Huddled like expectant kittens
The children retreat to the edge of the kitchen,
Peering from behind their huge, monastic dinner table.
Mother stands guard at the oven door,
The furious bread bubbling, beginning to rise.
Cautiously she sets out her mittens, pulls at the tip
Of the spatula, arranges an open space on the counter.
Her black bag of knives, sutures,
Clamps, probes and bandages waits.
It is time. The children inch closer
As the oven door is opened and the operation
To pull the boy from the pan begins.
The nascent hands are placed on the cookie sheet,
The small heart thumped into torturous beating.
Tangled blur of arms and legs,
The youngest child is sent upstairs
To fetch the apologetic seamstress.

BEAUTY AND THE BEAST

You come back from the afternoon like a priest.
The litanies fall behind you, cluttering
The doorstep, the walk. You hold your mouth
As though before you could think
An insult slithered out and fell short at my feet.
It is evening. Magics and religion,
Children and lizards, lie curled
At the stone steps of the door.
Inside, something sweats and stinks
Formless, pointing its naked red finger
Back towards the iron door, shouting
Through clenched teeth and choking fist
Something garbled, something
About the shape of the casserole,
The steam. And plates.

JEALOUSY

The intimate circuitry purrs at the edge of its box.
You wait while defiance fades: a wink, a click, a twist,
And all is off, all is done.
Yet each night you have the sensation
That nothing is as it was meant to be.
There is a light brush of air on your sleeping thigh.
A quick patter at your lips. The sheets of your bed
Move back and forth, or never
Are as they were when you first fell to sleep.
Carefully at midnight you have begun
To test the box, to pound its locked hinges, to feel
The hum of its outer plates. All
Is as it should be. Yet ...

Tonight there is an odd shuffling in the hall.
Something grates along the bulkhead. You stare
Into attentive dark and can almost see
Two eyes peering seductively back. Safe in her box
Your mechanical companion must lie
Switched off, awaiting without interest your morning needs. Yet,
The night smells of sympathetic perspiration
And one of you is in love.

THE ELITIST

What she said lay quietly in the street
And you could not hear the last of it.
Your own words barely stumbled off the tongue,
Fell into the gutter and rolled. The drain
Already half filled with speech your voice
Tottered in and was lost. Across the road
A man was yelling and the noise fell
Like stones, bouncing on concrete, solid against
The man's shoes. The directions to the Civic center
Curled on the pavement, collapsed from a youth's face.
A man ran from a bakery and behind him
The proprietor pointed and bubbled of words,
Dropping the stiff matter at the curb, in the cracks
Of metal grating. With arms and hands
You tried to make the woman understand,
With drawn eyes and twisted lips. She bent forward
As your obscenities clattered to the ground,
Rang flat like jar tops. A boy selling papers
Gave in and empty-mouthed pointed to print.
Language in the roads was almost a foot deep,
Driving a hazard. Crowds lifted their feet
Knee high and crunched verbs nouns
Adjectives to lifelessness, to quiet stone.
Morphemes rushing past caught in your pants,
Clung to a woman's skirt. A child
Having fashioned a raft of hard syllables
Floated along the crest, wild with the speed,
His own open mouth breeding greater depth

To the words running beneath him. Shop windows
Now are breaking; it is growing difficult
To stand against the flow. You and the woman
Are faltered against a wall, the current
Hitting you flush in the chest. Already
The bodies are moving in the rush, the ones
Drowned. You press both hands to the brick,
Holding to keep from being swept away.
You think uselessly of coming after us,
Those atop the light poles, shouting.

THE RAPTURE

When it is time to go they will go.
Instantaneously. Poof. Gone.
Flesh as light as down, clothes billowing.
Cars will come driverless off the road.
McClellan will put his tractor in the ditch
Trying to twist and look up
At the astonished bodies moving to Heaven.
Airplanes could drop down anyplace,
Slap into the Sound, or even plow up my corn.
The television will be frantic to stay on,
Technicians rushing about to replace
The hourly workers drifting through the roof;
If it's news time the anchormen
Will be trying to cover for one another,
Shifting from monitor to monitor. We've got
The ditch between us and the road
And that should stop any cars – but planes
I can't do much about. If it comes
At a critical time for the mill
I'll be able to pick up a little work
At damn good rate, filling in
Even though I know nothing. By then
Any body will be a good body.
This God-fearing county will most likely
For that day close up the liquor stores –
Just then, when people will be their driest.
Men engaged in collective occupations
Could be endangered when their brethren

Are snatched mid-effort up. You think
I'm some kind of pessimist, expect yourself
To be one moment standing, both hands
In dishwater, the next to be staring
Down at our roof, the water still crashing
From the backs of your hands. You go
If you like, but I come of commoner stuff.
To see you drifting off, a dot in a sky
With thousands of dots, might be hard:
But I feel safe enough, have my routine.
If you think it is time, try not
To leave the stove running, maybe hurry
And place a few sandwiches for me
In the refrigerator. And when you get
To second story or better, make noise,
Wave, let me know you're glad to be going.

FULL MOON

We sit alone, patient, at times
Making less noise than the trees.
The town would have it the other way.
Bloodhounds and rifles, the use of silver.
We could have had plenty of mutilated corpses,
Every high school boy too numb to smooth his way
Into one or another of his classmates would have been
Waiting in the bushes for likely projects,
Using twigs together to lay false tracks.
Your name could have been dragged torn through the streets
With a saving nod to your unbidden transmogrification.
Even now at our house they gather with tribal passions,
Defame the Cross, Christ, the pentagram.
What I think worries them most
In all this is my part. You would be glad
To go the normal course of events, have yourself
A bit of rage, let it be quickly over.
Your best suit and a quarter moon
I still think you would be their ritual,
Burn yourself out in a five-month or so.
I am an unnatural woman. I take
Your wolf's paw, talk as though you were listening.
At home the children I have had by you,
The ones I have yet to tell you of, suckle
Under the dog, whine and are licked clean.
The scent of your damp gray fur is in my nose
Like cotton, the air electric with your stupid
Courage. Husband, for my desires
They could pour your heart full of silver,
Go looking for someone else.

LIBERATION

It has come back with you from the lake.
You thought it would stay, peaceful
If not acquiescent, drifting at last to the bottom
Where the muck and mud would make of it nothing.
But here at seven a.m. in the mirror it is.
Its eyes wait for you to look the whole of it over.
Its mouth parts for your own unsolicited disbelief.
Down to breakfast it comes with you:
In a smooth plate it dares you to go away.
All morning you've heard it padding behind you,
Wiping its dirty shoes on the backs of your prints.
It has begun even to eat your shadow up.

It will not go much further. Back at the lake
You sit with the shore and stare at it,
A huge, gray cinderblock tied around its neck.
You must point out its dark bubbles as it goes down,
Remark its idiot terror at what surely is the proper thing to do.

EVOLUTION

The cats are coming down the street,
A populace of all colors, of a dozen
Lengths of hair, of infinite
Sound: cats, nonetheless. Filling the avenue
They stroll like a river, working
Inexorably in one direction – aimless,
Perhaps, but united in random nature.
The sound is unbelievable.
Paradoxically, the worst of the noise
Is the cheap bells some owners
Have placed about some cats' necks.
The mass is becoming so thick that,
Absurd though it is, there is a danger
Of being run down by a coterie so low to the ground.
Trashcans are overturned. Bicycles,
Housewares, are trodden flat in the road.
Everything has come to fear, save the rats:
In basements, in alleys, on balconies,
They rejoice – dancing arm in arm,
Tails wrapped about one another,
Gray blurs gathered in open sight.
In this alone there is hope.
Brother, you and I are but in the way.

THE LAST DINOSAUR

He's down in my basement.
For the lack of room the muscles
Have atrophied quite a bit, but still
He would impress anyone. Six times a day
I haul barrels of greens down the steps.
I keep the basement temperature controlled
Far better than I do the rest of the house.
And hauling out his excrement I cannot forget for long.
He brushes the underside of the floor above him,
Drinks his water as slowly as though
He enjoys the taste of it. I think
Now and again of calling in a paleontologist,
Of letting the world in on my treasure;
But there is something in the way he moves his head,
In the slow roll of his eyes, that stops me.
His brain the size of a walnut nonetheless
I believe he remembers the time when the planet
Belonged to him, size and sloth adequate.
Something about his great bulk, his ability
To barely lift the flat of his gut from the floor,
His quiet, deliberate movement, causes me to keep silence.
Our chemistries are the same. Amino acid
To amino acid we match as well as father and son.
I lie awake at night thinking of his ponderous form,
The last of its kind. The wife sleeps
Uncareful sleep, but his lowing stops me.
I believe at times he calls for me,
My shotgun, the few blasts that will put

All his species to extinction. But at times
I am sure he is calling for life, strong limbs
Beating the intransient forests to fear,
The flat of the sun warming his blood.
It is then that I believe in him most,
That when the wife comes down and says
Look, there is nothing here, that I can turn and say
Look, here is everything.

THE GIFT

The sparrows began this morning.
First one, then legions on the porch rail.
Yesterday it was the crows: quiet,
Angel-like, they circle the chimney.
All night the woodpeckers tapped staccato
Against the bedroom wall. A cardinal
Forced his way in through a hole in the floor
And two days now has been sitting on the couch.
I cannot even open the window to toss out bread
For fear more will find the way in.
Owls are massing on the fence; a hawk
Has position in the wood pile. All day
I can but serve tea to the reposed cardinal
And sit calmly in my corner, wings folded.
Already my hollow bones demand air:
Without the roof I might be
Nothing more than a spot against sky,
A communication between sagging branches.
I cannot yet let this envy go.

THE LOVE AFFAIR

The boy looks into the water and sees
Somehow the huge squid of *Twenty Thousand Leagues*
Under the Sea rising to enliven us.
As friendly and cold as the water is in daylight,
After dark the bottom drops away, the weeds
Could hold a man just inches from air.
He seems not to think about it until
At the edge of the yard, three feet from bulkhead,
He notices his mother and I have gone back,
Are blotted against the then small light
Limited to the porch. An opportunity for something
To reach just over the edge of the treated lumber
Marches up in him like the sound of rustling under the bed
And he is brave enough to back only another
Six feet in from the bank towards the house.
Fishing he lets his hand drag out through the grass,
Daytime is not as cautious about snakes as I would like him to be.
I catch him out on the end of the public pier
That should be torn down before someone
Too heavy cracks the lumber, is caught
With the splinters of wood in water too deep.
Night, and I almost love to see him shy away.
Myself, I've rowed out, a grown man, sat
In the middle of the boat, in the middle of the Sound,
Explained a patch of unevenness as the moon,
Stars, a crabber's marking of his pot. At times
I've thought I've seen my own father's bones
Climbing out of the water just where he left them,

Coming to tell me there are still places and things to fear.
Occasionally I'll sit out the full night on the water,
My son in the house with the sleep of stones,
Terrified at myself, and in love with the fact
That you can't see below the surface, can easily go there.
Staying in the boat is the best I can do.

CONTROL

Gravity is inspecting each part of you.
This is neither the time nor the place.
Your skirt hangs rigidly in position,
Stockings hold back your ebullient thighs.
The longings come and go like imaginary pains
Playing hide and seek in your bladder. Not here.
Gravity pulls at your flesh and your flesh,
Strained like twisted straw, resists.
Your shoes hold your feet in place; you keep
Your hands in your pockets. Weak skin
Yearns for earth. No. You lift your head
High in fragile air. Your eyes
Roll back. Were it not for your blouse
Your chest would break out and dance
With gravity in ecstatic swirls, lie
Sensuous and child-like on the ground. Gravity
Drums its fists along your cortex,
Fever like incubi races through your brain.
No. No. No. You are leaping,
Leaping. It is the last atrocity
For which you will be held responsible.

SELF-RESPECT

We can't get the deer off the front porch.
The birds are roosting in our closet
And they won't believe us when we aim
The air-rifle at the bases of their nests.
Morning we can't eat breakfast
For the squirrels that crawl up our shoulders,
Pull the food in mid-air from our forks.
It seems half the forest has moved in with us
And scream as I might they intend no leaving.
The wife for weeks has been hinting her father's shotgun,
Pointing at the key for the lock on the case.
Whacking the animals with a stick does nothing to move them:
We must brace our feet, shove with our thighs,
Getting in and out of the door, from room to room.
Our bed last week was taken by bears
And since then we have slept on hardwood floors.
The wife worries that in days she will be cooking for them,
Serving them on the patio and the coffee table.
I am almost ready for the gun, to draw my wife
Against the line of her suggestion. She would clean the corpse
If I make it. A bobcat curls in my favorite chair,
Absently watches the television. Why the woman does not know
I need a running target I'll never guess,
But on the floor our erotic spasms are more tactless and to the point
And I can see her leaping over hedges, racing along black fields,
Thick golden fur risen at the back of her neck.

Also by Ken Poyner

The Book of Robot, speculative poetry
Victims of a Failed Civics, speculative poetry
Constant Animals, flash fiction
Avenging Cartography, flash fiction
The Revenge of the House Hurlers, flash fiction
Engaging Cattle, flash fiction
Lessons from Lingering Houses, speculative poetry

Barking Moose Press

Look for them at bookstores and book sites everywhere, and www.barkingmoosepress.com.